Jasmine Green RESCUES
A Foal Called Storm

Helen Peters
illustrated by Ellie Snowdon

WALKER BOOKS

For Greta, Arthur, Polly, and Betsy
HP

For Clare x
ES

Text copyright © 2021 by Helen Peters
Illustrations copyright © 2021 by Ellie Snowdon

First US edition 2022
First published by Nosy Crow (UK) 2021

Library of Congress Catalog Card Number 2021947145
ISBN 978-1-5362-2271-5 (hardcover)
ISBN 978-1-5362-2272-2 (paperback)

22 23 24 25 26 27 TRC 10 9 8 7 6 5 4 3 2 1

Printed in Eagan, MN, USA

This book was typeset in Bembo.
The illustrations were done in pencil with a digital wash overlay.

Walker Books US
a division of
Candlewick Press
99 Dover Street
Somerville, Massachusetts 02144

www.walkerbooksus.com

Read all the books in the
Jasmine Green Rescues series

Oak Tree Farm

Truffle found this way →

← Willow found this way

← To village and school

Tom's house

Mistletoe raised this way ↓

To Mrs. Thomas's house
& Angus Mizon's farm

river

South
Downs

Ben's
house

Button
found here

Sky
found here

Chicken coop

Farmyard

Calf barn

Jasmine's
house

Holly
found here

Storm
found here

Lucky
born here

To Roger Turner's farm →

1

Where Have You Come From?

"That was a massive storm last night," said Jasmine to her sheepdog as she clambered over a fallen tree branch. "Did the thunder scare you, Sky?"

Sky leaped over the branch and ran along the riverbank, wagging his fluffy tail. If he had been frightened by the thunder, he showed no sign of it this morning.

It was the last Tuesday of May, and the school year had just finished. Jasmine had gotten up early, as usual, and had fed her other animals before walking Sky. She needed to be organized today because she had two rabbits coming to stay for the rest of the week.

Jasmine sometimes looked after other people's pets when they went on vacation. The money she made helped to pay for her animals' food. It was also good experience because she was planning to have an animal rescue center and boarding facility when she grew up.

They were almost back at the farmhouse when Jasmine heard a strange sound. Frowning in confusion, she stopped and listened.

The farm was full of noises: birds singing in the hedgerows, sheep baaing in the meadows, roosters crowing in the yard.

But this was different. It was a high-pitched whinny. None of the animals on Oak Tree Farm sounded like that.

Jasmine walked past the farmhouse toward the field called the Sixteen Acres, where the sound seemed to have come from. There were no animals there at the moment.

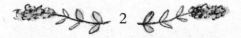

And then she stopped and stared in amazement.

Standing beside the hedge was a beautiful chestnut foal. It had a white blaze on its face and white socks on its hind legs. As Jasmine watched in awe, it lifted its head and gave another high-pitched whinny.

What was a foal doing there?

Jasmine's heart raced as the possibilities ran through her head. Her mom was a vet. Maybe she had brought the foal to the farm to recover after an illness or an operation. She had never done that before, but it was possible.

But if she had, then why hadn't she mentioned it? Suddenly a truly thrilling thought struck Jasmine.

What if the foal was a present? Had Mom and Dad actually bought her a foal of her own?

Her excitement drained away as she considered this in more detail. She already had two cats, a pig, a duck, a sheepdog, a ram, a deer, and a donkey. Apart from her cats, Toffee and Marmite,

Jasmine had rescued all these animals. And she had always had to convince her parents in order to keep them. Every time, they reminded her how many animals she already had, how much they cost to feed, how much space they needed, and how much time it took to look after them.

But Jasmine was an optimist. Although it was unlikely, it wasn't impossible. She clipped on Sky's leash and slowly approached the field.

The field gate was wide open, and suddenly Jasmine understood how ridiculous her hopes were. Even if her parents *had* bought her the foal, they certainly wouldn't have left it alone in a field with the gate open.

So whose was it, and where had it come from?

As she drew closer, she saw that something was very wrong.

The foal was soaking wet. It must have been out in that terrible storm that had blown through. The foal was shivering all over, which could have been from the cold, but looked more like fear.

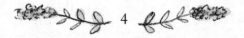 4

Its nostrils flared and quivered, and the whites of its eyes were showing. Its tail was clamped down against its body. Its ears swiveled rapidly, flicking back and forth, as though it was about to flee at any moment.

Jasmine stopped several yards away and spoke in a soft murmur, trying to soothe the little creature.

"What's wrong, little foal? Are you lost? Where's your mom?"

The foal was
beautiful, with
big dark eyes,
a short mane
and tail, and
long legs. As
Jasmine softly
approached, it
backed away,
terrified. She
noticed it was
limping.

"Oh! You're
hurt!"

There was a nasty cut on the foal's hind leg.
The gaping wound looked recent, and there was
a lot of dried blood around it.

"You poor thing. What happened to you?"

The wound looked deep enough to need
stitches. That was a job for Mom, but she was
out on an emergency call.

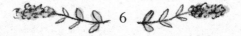

Jasmine thought quickly. An animal as nervous as this might bolt if anything startled it. She needed to keep the foal safe, but it was far too jumpy to let her approach it. She would just have to shut it in the field.

"I'm going to close this," she said as she walked slowly and quietly to the gate. "Don't worry, you're safe now. I'll look after you."

Jasmine had never cared for a foal before, but she had dealt with other frightened animals. She stood by the gate, speaking gently, trying to reassure the trembling creature.

"You're a boy, aren't you? I wonder what your name is. Do you even have a name? Are you an orphan? Are you hungry?"

If only Mom were here. But even if she were, she wouldn't be able to treat the foal's wound when he was this nervous. He would bolt if anyone went near him and probably give himself another injury.

Suddenly Jasmine knew what she needed to do.

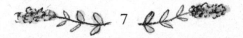

"I'll fetch some rails and build you a pen. That's what Mom does if she treats an animal in the field. And I'll phone Tom to come and help. He'll be so excited to meet you."

She took Sky back to the house and phoned Tom. He was Jasmine's best friend, and they had rescued many animals together. He lived very close to Oak Tree Farm, so he and Jasmine could walk to each other's houses.

"That's amazing," he said. "I'll come over right away."

Jasmine fetched metal rails from the lambing barn and carried them to the field one by one. As she approached the gate, the foal backed away, trembling. His ears were pinned back. Jasmine knew from experience with her donkey, Mistletoe, that this was another sign of anxiety.

When she opened the gate, the foal cocked his hind hoof, preparing to kick.

"Thanks for the warning," she said. "I'll stay far

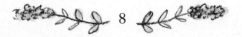

away from your back legs." As she carried the last rail in, Tom walked into the field.

"He's so beautiful!" he said. "I can't believe he just turned up here."

"I know. But he's so scared, poor baby. Look how he's shivering."

"Do you think he ran away? How did he get that horrible cut?"

"I don't know, but something bad must have happened to him. He's way too young to be away from his mom."

"Have you phoned the police?"

Jasmine didn't want to admit she hadn't thought of this. "Mom will phone them when she gets home," she said.

"Maybe he was abandoned," said Tom. "Or stolen."

"He can't have been stolen. If he was, the thieves would have him, wouldn't they? They wouldn't have left him here."

"Unless he escaped," said Tom.

While they constructed the pen, they talked softly to the foal, hoping to get him to relax and start to trust them.

"His coat's a lovely color," said Tom. "I like his white socks, too."

"And those cute little white markings on his forelegs, just above his hooves," said Jasmine.

By the time they'd finished, the foal had stopped trembling, but his mouth was tight and pinched and his body was still rigid with stress.

"How are we going to get him into the pen?" Tom asked.

"I'm not sure. When Mom treats foals, she always gets their mother to lead them in. They follow their moms anywhere."

"What about putting some food in there?"

"I don't know what to give him," said Jasmine. "He looks too young for solid food and I don't know if it's safe to give him cow's milk."

"Can you phone your mom?"

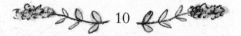

"Not really. She's probably delivering a calf right now."

From the orchard came a loud braying sound. The little foal pricked up his ears.

Tom's eyes widened. "What about Mistletoe?"

"To lead him into the pen?"

"Yes. Maybe the foal would follow him."

Jasmine looked doubtful. "He's not going to think Mistletoe's his mom."

"No, but horses and donkeys usually get along, don't they? Mr. Hobson said people have donkeys as companions for their horses, and some people use them as babysitters for foals."

Mr. Hobson was Mistletoe's previous owner, and he knew everything about donkeys.

"Well, if anyone can calm him down, it will be Mistletoe," said Jasmine. "He's the kindest donkey in the whole world."

2
A Good Sign

Mistletoe was browsing in the orchard with Jasmine's pet deer, Dotty. Jasmine fetched his halter and lead rope.

"Hello, Mistletoe," she said. "There's somebody we'd like you to meet."

She held out the halter so the donkey could sniff it. He was used to wearing it, but it was good manners to warn him before she slipped it over his head.

Mistletoe was twenty years old and very patient and calm. Jasmine had no worries about his behavior, but she wasn't sure how the foal would react to him.

When the foal saw Mistletoe approaching the field, he froze, staring at the small brown donkey. Mistletoe stared back. The foal lifted his head, gave a loud snort, and shied away.

Jasmine and Tom exchanged worried glances.

"Should we take Mistletoe back to the orchard?" asked Tom.

But Jasmine was reluctant to give up so soon. "I think they'll be fine. They can stay away from each other if they want to. I'll just leave Mistletoe's halter on in case we need to catch him quickly."

Mistletoe walked calmly into the field. He wasn't looking at the foal, but Jasmine had learned to read the language of his ears. His left ear was trained on Jasmine, but his right ear was swiveling around in the direction of the foal.

The foal stood facing away from them. As Jasmine watched, he turned his head to look at Mistletoe.

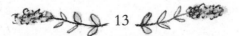

"He's curious," she said. "That must be a good sign."

"I guess we should give them time to get to know each other," said Tom.

Jasmine unclipped Mistletoe's lead rope and sat on the grassy bank at the edge of the field to watch the animals.

"The foal is so gorgeous, isn't he?" she said. "He's got such a cute face and such beautiful eyes."

"We should give him a name," said Tom. "Just for the time he's with us, I mean. We can't keep calling him 'the foal.'"

"How about Storm?" Jasmine suggested. "He arrived in a storm, and he's probably had a stormy life, poor little thing."

"That suits him," said Tom. "What do you think, Storm?"

Mistletoe looked toward the foal, who had walked farther off and was facing the other way. Mistletoe stared at him for a few seconds and then wandered off in the opposite direction.

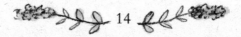

Storm turned to face Mistletoe. He stared at the donkey, took a few steps forward, and then stopped and turned away.

Mistletoe turned to look at the foal again. He ambled slowly toward him. He stopped several yards away and looked directly at him. Storm returned his look.

"Aren't Harry's rabbits coming today?" asked Tom, sitting on the bank beside Jasmine. "Ugh, this grass is soaking wet."

"Yes, he's bringing them at eleven."

"Have you told your parents they're house rabbits yet?"

"Not exactly. Actually, I think they've forgotten they're coming. I asked them ages ago, and I haven't exactly reminded them."

"They won't mind, though, will they? They're such cute rabbits. You'll just have to keep the living-room door shut when they're out of their hutch, in case the cats get in."

"The cats aren't allowed in the living room

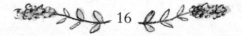

anyway," said Jasmine, "after they scratched the furniture. Mom and Dad would be fine with the rabbits normally, but Auntie Evil's coming today, and she hates animals."

"Is she the one who said your cats should be put down?"

"Yes. She's horrible. But she's Dad's auntie so he invites her to stay sometimes. I don't know why he bothers; she spends the whole time moaning about everything."

"Look," said Tom, pointing at the animals.

Mistletoe was standing close to Storm. The little foal took a few tentative steps toward him. Then, to Jasmine's delight, he walked right up to Mistletoe and sniffed his face. Mistletoe stood perfectly still while Storm sniffed around his mouth and nose.

Jasmine held her breath. This was a really important process. Animals got to know each other mainly by smell.

Mistletoe let Storm sniff him for a while, then

 17

turned and walked away. Storm stayed completely still, his big eyes fixed on the donkey.

A few minutes later, Mistletoe ambled back toward the foal. Storm sniffed his face again. This time, Mistletoe sniffed him in return. Once he had explored the foal's face, he sniffed his mane, withers, and back. Then he walked away. Storm followed him.

Mistletoe broke into a trot. Storm watched him trotting around the edge of the field, then he started limping after the donkey. Mistletoe turned around and trotted after Storm.

"Look!" exclaimed Jasmine. "They're playing together! They must be making friends."

The animals slowed to a walk, some distance apart from each other. Jasmine heard a vehicle pull into the farmyard.

"Oh, good, Mom's back," she said, walking to the gate.

But it wasn't her mom's car. It was a big shiny pickup truck. The passenger door opened and Harry got out.

"Oh, no! They're early. I won't be able to warn Mom."

"Maybe that's better," said Tom. "If the rabbits are already in the living room when your mom gets back, she can't really say no, can she?"

3
Buster and Daisy

Tom stayed with Mistletoe and Storm while Jasmine went to greet Harry.

"You must be Jasmine," said Harry's dad, who was lifting things out of the truck bed. "I'm Adam. I'm afraid there's a lot of stuff. I hope you've got a big living room."

"Quite big," said Jasmine. Then she walked around to the back of the truck and her mouth fell open in shock.

"It's a two-tier hutch," said Mr. Adam. "And

these railings clip together to make the playpen."

"Wow," said Jasmine. "Where are the rabbits?"

Harry took a carrying case from the back seat. "Here."

Having seen the vast two-story cage and the huge number of playpen pieces, Jasmine expected the rabbits to be enormous. So she was surprised to find a pair of tiny little bunnies peering out at her. They had long floppy ears, fluffy golden fur, shining dark eyes, and little twitching noses.

"Oh, they're so cute! Are they babies?"

"No," said Harry, "but Miniature Lops always look like babies."

"They're gorgeous. What are their names?"

"Buster and Daisy. They're a boy and girl, but they've both been neutered."

"Leave them in the car while we set everything up," said Mr. Adam. "Where should we take the supplies, Jasmine?"

Jasmine picked up a stack of playpen segments. "I'll show you."

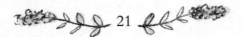

It took a long time to set it all up. The giant two-story cage sat inside the playpen, which was three feet high. It took up half the living room, so they had to move all the furniture into the other half. By the time they'd finished, there was barely room for a person to squeeze between the furniture.

Jasmine's stomach squirmed as she looked at the rearranged room. It was great that the rabbits had so much space, but she wasn't looking forward to the moment when her mom walked in.

After they had fetched the toys, tunnels, nesting boxes, water bottles, food, hay, rubber matting, and litter tray, they went back to get the rabbits. Mom drove into the farmyard as Harry lifted the carrier out. Jasmine could tell from her puzzled face that she hadn't remembered they were coming.

"Hello, Nadia," said Mr. Adam. "Thanks so much for looking after the rabbits."

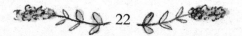

Mom's face cleared. "Oh, you're very welcome. Jasmine will do all the work anyway." She looked into the carrier. "What gorgeous little bunnies! Do you want a hand with their hutch?"

"No, everything's done. Jasmine's been very helpful."

"Great," said Mom, taking two bags of groceries from the car. "I would invite you in, but Michael's aunt's arriving any minute and I haven't tidied up yet. She's very particular about tidiness, and our house is a terrible disappointment to her."

"I hope she won't mind the rabbits," said Mr. Adam.

"Oh, no, it's fine. She probably won't even see them. She doesn't go outside much."

"Oh, but they're—"

"I'll take the rabbits," said Jasmine, almost snatching the carrier from Harry. "Thank you so much. Have a lovely vacation."

"Wonderful to see you," said Mom, hurrying inside with the groceries.

Mr. Adam gave Jasmine a quizzical look. "Your mom does know they're house rabbits, doesn't she?"

"She probably just forgot," said Jasmine. "She's very forgetful."

She waved Mr. Adam and Harry off and took the rabbits inside. Hopefully Mom wouldn't come into the living room for a while.

Jasmine carefully lifted Daisy out of the case. "You're so warm and soft," she said, stroking her golden fur and floppy ears. "I'll pop you in the hutch, and you can explore when you're ready."

She took Buster out. He had a white stripe down the middle of his face, so it was easy to tell them apart.

She decided to tell Mom about the foal first and deal with the rabbits later. After all, the foal needed urgent treatment, whereas the rabbits were safe and happy.

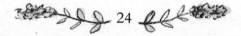

Mom was in the kitchen, wiping the drainboard.

"Have you gotten the rabbits settled?" she asked.

"Yes, they're fine," Jasmine said. "There's another thing, though. I know you're busy, but it's urgent."

Mom turned around. "Oh?"

"It's a foal."

"A foal? What do you mean? Where?"

Jasmine explained. Mom looked slightly dazed.

"How extraordinary. I wonder where he came from. I'll have to phone around and make inquiries."

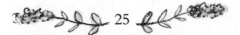

"The problem is, he's got a nasty cut on his leg. Do you think you might be able to treat it?"

Mom glanced anxiously at the clock. "I will, obviously, but Auntie Eva will also be here any minute now, and the place is a mess."

"I'll help you," said Jasmine.

Mom smiled at her. "That's very kind. Tell you what, I'll get her settled with a cup of tea and then I'll come and look at this foal. She always likes to have a rest when she arrives, and Dad should be back soon anyway. At least the living room's tidy. She can have her tea in there."

"Maybe she'd like it in her bedroom," suggested Jasmine hopefully. "I could take it up to her."

"No, I don't want her going upstairs yet. I haven't made her bed. I'll just take these flowers into the living room."

"Let me take them," urged Jasmine.

"No, the vase is really heavy."

Jasmine watched helplessly as her mother

carried the flowers across the hall. "Open the door for me, would you?" she called.

Feeling sick with dread, Jasmine crossed the hall and opened the living-room door. There was nothing she could do. She would have to face her mother's fury.

4
Auntie Evil

Mom stared at the rabbit hutch and the enormous playpen. Then she turned to Jasmine, her face tight with anger.

"Jasmine. What on *earth* have you done?"

"They're house rabbits," said Jasmine, trying to keep her voice normal. "I told you that, didn't I?"

"No," snapped Mom. "You did not. How could you do this? You know Auntie Eva hates animals inside the house. She makes enough fuss about the cats. And look at the state of this room! There's not even space to sit down."

"I'm really sorry. Maybe we can put the sofa in the hall?"

Mom shot Jasmine a withering look. "You'll just have to move the rabbits. I'll keep Auntie Eva in the kitchen until you're done."

"Where? I can't take them outside. I asked Harry and he said even in the summer a sudden move outside can send them into shock from stress. Rabbits can die of shock. And what if there's another thunderstorm? Loud noises can send them into shock, too. And their hutch isn't an outdoor hutch, and—"

The ringing of the doorbell cut through her words.

"Just get rid of all this, please, and no more arguments," said Mom. "Put them in your bedroom if you can't take them outside."

"But there's not enough space in my bedroom."

"Well, make some space, then."

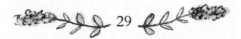

Mom went to open the front door. "Hello, Auntie Eva!" Jasmine heard her say in a falsely bright voice. "How lovely to see you. Come in. Let me take your suitcase. How was your journey?"

"Terrible," said Auntie Eva. Jasmine could smell her heavy perfume from the living room. "The train was filthy and the taxi cost an absolute fortune."

"Oh, dear," said Mom. "I'm sorry I couldn't meet you at the station. I had an emergency calving."

"Yes, well, that's the trouble with working mothers. Family always comes last."

"I do put my family first," said Mom, "and so does Michael, but sometimes we have to deal with emergencies."

"Oh, I wouldn't expect Michael to pick me up! He does quite enough already, poor man."

"Well, I'll give you the money for the taxi," said Mom.

"It's not about the money. Can I come in and

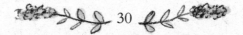

sit down? I'm exhausted. And a cup of tea would be nice."

"Of course. Come into the kitchen."

"No, I'll sit in the living room. Your kitchen chairs are very uncomfortable."

Oh, no, thought Jasmine. *Not the living room.*

But Mom just said, "Whichever you like. I'll make the tea."

Jasmine walked to the doorway and forced a smile. Auntie Eva gave her a disapproving look. She wore a long black fur-trimmed coat, a brightly patterned silk scarf, and dark-red lipstick.

"Hello, Jasmine. You've grown. Your hair needs cutting. I hope you haven't been sitting on the sofa in those muddy pants."

"No," said Jasmine.

Auntie Eva walked past her into the room and then recoiled in horror.

"*What* is *that*?"

"It's a rabbit hutch."

"In the living room? Why?"

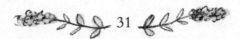

"They're house rabbits."

"House rabbits!" Auntie Eva backed out of the room in disgust. "That's absolutely revolting. How can anybody use the living room when it's full of rodents?"

She stalked across the hall into the kitchen. Jasmine followed dejectedly.

"You'll have to bring a comfortable chair in here for me, Nadia, until you've moved those creatures out and fumigated the room. They're bound to have fleas. Surely Michael doesn't approve."

"Jasmine's looking after them for her friend," said Mom.

"*Why?*"

"Because Jasmine's very good with animals. People pay her to look after their pets."

Auntie Eva shuddered. "I wouldn't let other people's pets anywhere near my house. They're probably carrying all sorts of diseases. Go and take the rabbits outside, Jasmine, like a good girl."

"They're house rabbits," said Mom. "They can't live outside."

Jasmine stared at her mother in amazement.

"Don't be ridiculous," said Auntie Eva. "Of course rabbits live outside."

"Well, these don't. They're lovely rabbits and they're very clean. I'm sure you'll enjoy their

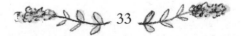

company once you get used to them. Now, I'm afraid I'm going to have to pop out to the field to see to a foal with an injured leg. Michael should be back soon to look after you."

"If it has an injured leg, it will have to be put down," Auntie Eva called after Mom and Jasmine as they escaped to the mudroom to put their boots on. "There's nothing you can do for a horse once its leg is injured. Best to shoot it immediately."

Mom grabbed her medical bag and closed the kitchen door. "Come on, Jasmine. Let's go look at this foal."

5
Somebody's Bound to Know Something

When Mom saw the foal, her tense expression softened. "Oh, what a beautiful little creature!"

They watched as Storm walked toward Mistletoe. Tom was still sitting on the bank.

Storm put his mouth close to Mistletoe's face, pulled back his lips, and started clacking his teeth and champing. Mistletoe drew his head back slightly, then moved it closer again, allowing Storm to continue.

"What's Storm doing?" asked Jasmine anxiously.

"It's something foals do to older horses," said Mom. "He's telling Mistletoe that Mistletoe's the boss and he will submit to him."

"Wow. So they're bonding."

"That was a great idea to bring Mistletoe in," said Mom. "Now we just need him to lead the foal into the pen."

Jasmine picked up Mistletoe's lead rope and walked slowly toward him.

The animals had moved apart,
but Mistletoe's right ear was trained
on Storm. "Would you come and stand
in that pen for a little while?" she asked
Mistletoe, holding out the lead rope for
him to sniff.

Mistletoe plodded patiently up the field
beside her. Jasmine glanced back.

Storm was standing very still, looking at
the donkey. When they had almost reached

the pen, she saw, to her delight, that Storm was limping through the field toward them.

She led Mistletoe into the pen and tied his lead rope lightly to the top bar. "Would you mind staying in here to look after Storm while Mom stitches his cut?" she asked him.

Mistletoe stood calmly in the pen. Jasmine scratched his withers and behind his ears. Then she left the pen, keeping one rail open, and sat next to Tom.

Storm stood nearby, watching the donkey.

"Come on, Storm," Jasmine pleaded. "Come into the pen."

"It's no use being impatient," said Mom. "Let him do it in his own time. I'll text Dad and ask him to pick up some mare's milk replacement while he's out. The foal must be hungry."

"How old do you think he is?" asked Jasmine.

"I'd say not more than three weeks. I'll be able to tell when I look inside his mouth. Foals get their first teeth at a week old, and then they keep getting more until they have a full set at nine months."

"Do you think he ran away?" asked Tom.

Mom shook her head. "A foal this age would never leave its mother on purpose."

"So he's been abandoned?"

"It looks like it. Male foals—colts—are more likely to be abandoned than fillies, since they can't produce more foals."

Jasmine was outraged. "How could anyone abandon a foal?"

"Sometimes people get a horse and don't realize how expensive it is to keep. Then the horse has a foal and they can't afford to look after it. Or it gets injured, like this one, and they can't afford the vet's bills."

"Then they should send it to an animal sanctuary."

"Of course they should, but sometimes they're too embarrassed to admit they can't afford it."

"But to just dump him in a field! That's so cruel!"

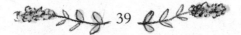 39

"Yes, it is," said Mom. "It's lucky he found us."

Jasmine stared at her. "Do you mean he's ours now? We get to keep him?"

"No, of course not. We need to find out who he belongs to. I just meant it's lucky he ended up in a place where there's a vet and a girl who loves looking after animals."

Jasmine gasped. She gazed, wide-eyed, at her mother.

"What if they abandoned him here *on purpose*? What if it's someone who knows we've rescued other animals, so they knew the foal would be going to a good home? Like in Victorian times, when poor mothers left their babies outside an orphanage so they'd be taken care of."

"I suppose it's possible. But he could have just been dumped on the road and made his way to the field. As soon as I've sedated him, I'll scan him for a microchip. If he has one, that will tell us who he belongs to."

"Look," said Tom. "He's going in."

"Oh, well done, Storm," said Jasmine delightedly as he limped into the pen. "Good boy."

Storm stood beside Mistletoe and sniffed his face. Then he made the teeth-clacking sounds again. Jasmine gently closed the rail.

"Great work, you two," said Mom. "Now you'll need to keep him still while I sedate him, Jasmine."

"Should I take Mistletoe out?"

"No, being close to him will help the foal feel safe. We want to restrain him as little as possible and let them interact. First you need to get the foal used to your presence. Go into the pen, but stay away from his hind legs. Stand on his left-hand side, so you don't get between him and Mistletoe. Just talk to him, and let him make the first contact. Once he's sniffed you and seems comfortable, you can stroke him gently, to get him used to your touch. There's no hurry. I'll do some emails while I'm waiting."

"What should I do?" asked Tom.

"Can you fetch the hose from the orchard? We'll need to wash his wound. Thanks, Tom."

Jasmine climbed quietly into the pen, speaking softly to the animals. Storm had one ear trained on her and one on Mistletoe. After several minutes, Storm bent to sniff her hand. Jasmine beamed.

"Good boy. You're so gorgeous."

Talking quietly to him, she kept her arm still

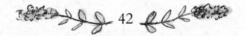

while he sniffed it. When he seemed comfortable, she softly stroked his shoulders. Storm stiff-
ened slightly, but he didn't move away or cock
his hoof. Jasmine stroked his withers, back, and
ribs. "You're so lovely, Storm. How could anyone
have abandoned you? Where did you come from?

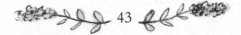

You must be missing your mom so much. Don't worry, we'll find her." She stroked his soft cheeks.

"He's really trusting you," said Mom. "That's great. Now put your left arm around his chest and gently lift his tail with the other hand. That should stop him from trying to jump or run away."

Storm stood still as Jasmine held him. Mom inserted a syringe into his mouth and pushed the plunger.

"The sedative will keep him calm, but he'll still be conscious and standing up. It will take about half an hour to start working. Just keep stroking him while I scan him for a microchip."

"Does it hurt animals to have a microchip put in them?" asked Tom, setting the running hose down beside the pen.

"No, it's only the size of a grain of rice, and you can give them a local anesthetic before you implant it, so they don't feel a thing."

Mom ran the scanner along Storm's neck, hovering it a few inches from his body. If he had a microchip, the scanner would beep and a long number would show up on the screen. When Mom entered the number into a database, it would give her all Storm's details.

The scanner stayed silent. Mom scanned him again, but nothing happened.

"That's a shame," she said. "But lots of owners wait until their foal's a few months old before they get it done."

"So how do we find his owner?" asked Jasmine.

"I'll send his photo to the police and all the local vets and stables. Somebody's bound to know something."

6
We'll Always Look After You

Once the sedative had relaxed Storm, Mom gave him a health check to see whether he was well enough to have a local anesthetic before she stitched his wound. Jasmine stroked him while Mom checked his eyes and ears. Then Mom gently opened his mouth.

"This is how you age a foal. See his central incisors? Two in the upper jaw and two in the lower jaw. Foals get those at a week old. And Storm also has three premolars just appearing, see there? Those come through at two weeks. When he's a month old, he'll get his second incisors, but there's no sign of those yet."

"So he's between two weeks and a month old," said Tom.

"Yes, but since the premolars are only just appearing, I'd say closer to two weeks. Far too young to leave his mom. Foals generally stay with their mothers for six months."

"Maybe his mom died," said Tom. "And his owners didn't want to take care of him."

"Perhaps," said Mom. She took her stethoscope from its case to listen to Storm's heart.

"His heartbeat's a bit fast, but that's probably due to stress, poor thing. I'll give him an anesthetic and treat that leg. Can you hold him gently, Jasmine, in case he reacts to the needle?"

Mom was very skilled at giving injections, and Storm didn't react at all. "Now you can flush his wound out, Tom," she said, "while we wait for the anesthetic to work."

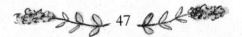

Tom let the water run gently over the wound until all the dirt and caked blood was washed away. Mom rinsed it with diluted disinfectant to kill off any infection, and then she crouched down to examine it.

"It's quite deep, but it hasn't gone through to the tendon or bone, thank goodness. Hopefully it won't cause any lasting damage, but it's certainly enough to frighten someone into dumping him."

Jasmine stroked Storm and talked softly to him while Mom stitched his wound.

"You're so brave, Storm," she murmured. "And so patient."

As Mom finished bandaging the wound to protect the stitches, Jasmine heard her dad's truck pull into the farmyard. Seconds later, Mom's phone pinged with a text. She looked at the screen.

"Dad's got the mare's milk replacement. You'd better come and mix some up, Jasmine. And I need to get lunch."

"Should I stay with Storm?" asked Tom.

"That would be great. You've got your phone, don't you? Call me if there's any problem."

In the farmyard, Dad and Manu were unloading the truck.

"So you've stolen a foal now, Jasmine?" Dad said.

"I didn't steal him!"

He gave her a mock-serious look. "Are you sure? It seems rather convenient that a foal just turns up in our field, needing to be looked after."

"Exactly! So maybe someone brought him here on purpose. Because they couldn't take care of him but they knew we would."

"Well," he said, "stranger things have happened."

"Your aunt's arrived, Michael," said Mom.

"Ah," said Dad. He didn't look enthusiastic, but he walked into the kitchen with the children and said, "Hello, Auntie Eva! How nice to see you."

"Oh, Michael, you look exhausted. Come and sit down. Where's Nadia? You need a cup of tea."

"I'm fine, honestly. And I can make my own tea."

"Well, I'm sure you've had plenty of practice. No wonder you're exhausted. I gather you've had to look after Manu all morning, too. Why are you scratching your head, Manu? Do you have lice?"

Manu stopped scratching his head.

"There's a hole in your pants," said Auntie Eva. "Your mother ought to patch that."

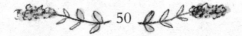

"I like holes," muttered Manu.

"What did you say? You need to speak up."

Mom came in and opened the fridge.

"Have you washed your hands, Nadia, before you handle food?" asked Auntie Eva.

"Yes, thank you, Auntie, I have. I'll make lunch after I've helped Jasmine mix up the foal's milk."

"Oh, it's still alive, is it?" asked Auntie Eva.

"Very much so."

"I'll get lunch ready," said Dad.

"Do you have to do the cooking, too, Michael?" said Auntie Eva. "You poor man."

"I like cooking," Dad said.

"I would help, of course," said Auntie Eva, "but I've just had a manicure and I can't risk chipping the polish."

Jasmine glanced in distaste at Auntie Eva's long, red, witchy nails. She followed Mom to the mud-room and shut the door.

"Why is she like that?" asked Jasmine.

"Like what?"

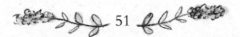

"So sexist. Always saying Dad shouldn't be doing the cooking and stuff."

Mom sighed. "Different generation, I suppose. I don't think her husband helped in the house, and she seems to feel that's how things should be. Not that it made her happy."

"But that doesn't make sense," said Jasmine.

"Well, people don't always make sense, unfortunately. And Auntie Eva was sent to boarding school when she was very young, so she grew up with very different rules. All right, let's mix up a bucket of milk."

"A bucket? I thought we'd be bottle-feeding him."

"No, it's much better to get him used to a bucket. It will save you a lot of time and lost sleep. It's better for the foal, too. He can just drink a little at a time, like he would from his mother. If they guzzle it all at once from a bottle, it can give them an upset stomach."

"How much do we give him?"

"He should drink about a quarter of his body weight each day. I'll have to estimate his body weight."

"Wow, that sounds like a lot," said Jasmine, trying to imagine how high her plate would be piled if she were to eat a quarter of her body weight.

"Dip your finger into the milk and let him suck it," said her mother. "Once he's doing that, lift the bucket toward his muzzle and gradually immerse your finger in the bucket. When you take your finger away, hopefully he'll drink from the bucket."

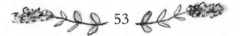

"And if he doesn't?"

"Keep trying until he does. He's probably hungry, so he shouldn't take too long to learn."

Jasmine checked on the rabbits, who were playing tug-of-war with a chew toy. She watched them for a minute, smiling at their cuteness, and then she took Storm's milk to the Sixteen Acres.

"I bet you'd love a bucket of milk, wouldn't you, Mistletoe?" said Tom as he led the donkey out of the pen. Mistletoe stood on the other side of the rails and leaned his head over to sniff the little foal.

Jasmine dipped her finger into the milk and lifted it to Storm's mouth. "Here you are, Storm. Nice warm milk."

He didn't open his mouth, so she wiped some milk between his lips to give him a taste.

Storm sniffed her finger. She gently placed it in his mouth and he started to suck it. Jasmine smiled with delight.

"Good boy, Storm. Well done. Can you hold the bucket up to his muzzle, Tom?"

Storm sucked her finger as Tom lifted the bucket. Jasmine gradually lowered her finger into the milk. Storm carried on sucking her finger. "There's no more milk there," she said. "You need to drink from the bucket."

But Storm still sucked hopefully on her finger. Jasmine took it away and dipped it into the milk. She offered it to him again and he sucked it eagerly. She lowered her finger into the bucket. Again, Storm just sucked on her finger. When she took it out of his mouth, he didn't drink from the bucket but tried to suck her finger again.

"All the milk's in the bucket, look," she said.

She tried again, but he still just wanted to suck her finger.

"Poor Storm," said Jasmine, stroking his face sadly. "You're used to feeding from your mom, aren't you? You don't want to drink from a

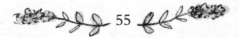

bucket." She turned to Tom, her eyebrows drawn together in anger. "Can you believe anybody would just abandon a tiny little foal? They must be so evil."

Tom looked worried. "What if he refuses to drink? Baby animals die without their mothers."

Jasmine put her arms around Storm and kissed the top of his head. "We won't let that happen. We'll keep trying until he drinks. Don't worry, Storm. If we can't find your mom, we'll always look after you. You'll never be abandoned again, I promise."

7
It's Your Fault

Much to Jasmine's annoyance, Mom insisted she go inside for lunch.

"You're so lucky, staying in the field with Storm," she said to Tom. "Hopefully I won't have to stay too long. I'll bring you some sandwiches."

She trudged back to the house. As soon as she opened the door from the garden into the hall, Mom called, "Is that you, Jasmine? Can you find Manu and ask him to wash his face and hands? And clean yourself up, too."

Jasmine made a face. Mom and Dad weren't usually that fussy. This was all because of Auntie Evil.

She was heading upstairs when Manu walked out of the living room. In his arms was a fluffy golden rabbit.

"Manu! Put her back!"

"It's fine. She's completely safe."

"Where's Buster? You haven't let him out, have you?"

"Stop panicking. He's in the hutch."

Jasmine shook her head. "Anyway, it's lunchtime. Put Daisy back."

She followed Manu into the living room. The rabbits had eaten all their food, so she stretched over an armchair for the bag of pellets that she'd put on the mantel. As she reached out for it, she knocked over a large glass-framed photo. With a shriek of alarm, she grabbed it just before it crashed to the floor.

"Oh, no!" exclaimed Manu, rushing to the doorway. "Look what you did!"

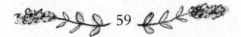

Jasmine turned. To her horror, Manu's arms were empty.

"What have you done? Where is she?"

"She jumped out of my arms and ran into the hall. It's your fault. She jumped when you screamed."

Jasmine barged past him into the hall. At the sight of the door to the garden, she turned cold all over.

"Oh, no, oh, no!"

She had left the door wide open.

"Jasmine, Manu!" called Mom. "Lunch is ready."

"What do we do?" whispered Manu, wide-eyed with worry.

"We'll look until we find her. Don't tell anyone. I don't think she'd have gone outside. She's a

house rabbit. She'll be hiding inside somewhere."

"But what if she did go outside?"

Jasmine thought quickly. "We'll leave her carrier in the garden with food in it, and she'll go into it."

"But what if she doesn't?"

"She will," Jasmine insisted. "She won't want to be outside alone."

The kitchen door opened. "Manu, Jasmine, will you come in for lunch, for goodness' sake?" said Mom. "What on earth have you been doing? Have you even washed up? You don't look like you have."

"Sorry," said Jasmine. "Coming."

They followed Mom into the kitchen. Auntie Eva looked at them in distaste.

"It's the height of bad manners to keep people waiting at the table. My children would never have disobeyed me like that."

I bet they wouldn't, thought Jasmine as she and Manu went to wash their hands in the mudroom. *You'd probably have grounded them if they had.*

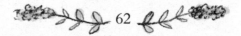

"Eat quickly, then we'll start looking," she whispered to Manu. "You search the garden and I'll do the house."

Toffee and Marmite were curled up together in their basket. "Sorry you've been banished out here," said Jasmine, stroking

them as they purred with pleasure. "It won't be for long."

She couldn't bear to imagine what might happen if the cats found Daisy. As they walked back into the kitchen, she said, "Can everyone remember to keep the mudroom door shut so the cats can't get out?"

Mom was ladling out the soup. "The police just phoned," she said. "They've had a call from someone in Ryewell who's concerned about the

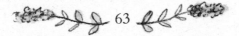

stables next door to their house. They've reported the owner for neglecting his horses."

"That's awful!" said Jasmine. "Do they think Storm came from there?"

"They don't know yet, but they've passed the information to the RSPCA, and the RSPCA is going to inspect the stables tomorrow."

"Poor Storm, if he came from somewhere where they mistreat their horses," said Jasmine.

Auntie Eva was inspecting her soupspoon. "This isn't quite clean," she said. "Could I have another one?"

A look of irritation passed over Dad's face as he got up and fetched another spoon.

"Oh, not you, dear, I meant Nadia," said Auntie Eva. "You shouldn't have to do everything. Manu, take your elbows off the table. Jasmine, don't slurp your soup."

What with worrying about Daisy, worrying about Storm not feeding, and Auntie Eva's constant stream of comments, lunchtime seemed like

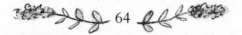

an eternity to Jasmine. Normally she loved dessert, but when Dad brought out meringues and cream, she felt as though she would burst with frustration if she had to stay one moment longer.

"I'm not hungry," she said. "Can I take Tom's sandwiches out? He must be starving."

"Fine," said Mom, "but come straight back. You've hardly seen Auntie Eva and I'm sure she'd like to spend some time with you. I'll go and check on Storm as soon as we've finished lunch."

Auntie Eva tutted. "My children would never have been allowed to leave the table before the end of a meal."

Maybe that's why your children moved to Australia, thought Jasmine as she thankfully made her escape.

8
Completely Ruined

"I've been trying nonstop, but he won't feed from the bucket," said Tom. "And he must need milk. What if he pines to death?"

Jasmine put his packed lunch on the grass. "I'll try while you eat."

Tom climbed out of the pen and Jasmine climbed in. She kissed Storm's head and stroked his mane and withers.

"You want your mom, don't you? You don't want to drink from a bucket. But it's nice milk,

Storm, and you really need to drink. Just try it."

Storm eagerly sucked milk from her finger, but he still wouldn't drink from the bucket. Jasmine kept encouraging him as she told Tom the terrible news about Daisy.

"Should I go and look for her?" he asked.

"No, I have to go back in a minute, so you'll need to stay with Storm. They're making me sit with Auntie Evil, but I'll try to escape and look for Daisy."

Storm was sucking from her finger. She lowered it into the milk. And this time, Storm started to drink from the bucket.

"Oh, well done, Storm! You've got it!"

Tom beamed. "That's amazing! I thought he'd never do it."

"Clever boy," said Jasmine. "You're an angel, Storm."

They watched in delight as Storm drank the milk. "Dad said we can make a little pen in Mistletoe's shelter in the orchard," said Jasmine. "So Storm can be close to Mistletoe at night."

"What about Dotty and Truffle? Do deer and pigs get along with foals?"

"Mom says horses and deer often graze together and share water troughs. And there's a farm she visits where pigs and horses share a field and they get along fine. Apparently some horses are scared of pigs, but Truffle's such a nice pig, I'm sure she'll be kind to Storm."

"Should we make the pen now?" asked Tom.

"No, I've got to go or Mom will be mad. I hope Manu found Daisy."

Storm took his head out of the bucket.

"Don't you want more?" Tom asked. "You haven't drunk much."

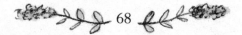

But although they encouraged him all they could, Storm wouldn't drink any more.

"I'll keep trying," said Tom. "He must still be hungry."

Jasmine headed back to the house. In the garden, Manu's legs were sticking out from under a bush.

"No luck?" she asked.

Manu wriggled out. "Nope. But I put the pet carrier over there with some carrots inside it, so hopefully she'll smell them and come back."

"I'm sure she will if she's out here," said Jasmine. "She won't want to be out alone at night."

Horrible visions crowded into her head of all the things that could happen at night to a helpless rabbit. She pushed them away.

"I've got to go and sit with Auntie Evil," she said, "but I'll get away as soon as I can."

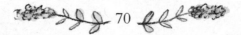

Auntie Eva had been droning on for what felt like several hours. Jasmine wasn't listening. Her head was filled with worry. What if there was a fox around? What if Daisy never came back? What if she died from shock?

Auntie Eva took a sip of water. "How are you doing in French, Jasmine?"

"Uh, we don't do much French. We've learned the days of the week, and the numbers up to ten."

"Oh, dear, that's terrible. Both my children were fluent in French by your age. But of course they went to a very good school."

As she proceeded to list her children's endless

achievements, Jasmine sank lower in her chair so she could look under the sofa. *Please,* she thought, *please let Daisy be safe inside.*

"Ariadne was the youngest girl in her school ever to earn top honors on piano," Auntie Eva was saying. "Don't slouch, Jasmine. You'll have terrible posture. Do you play any instruments?"

"Not really," said Jasmine, leaning her head to one side to get a better look under the sideboard. "I played the recorder in first grade, but I gave it up."

Auntie Eva tutted. "That's the problem with modern parents—they let their children give up far too easily."

"They wanted me to give up. They said my playing gave them headaches."

"Oh, that is shocking. I remember when Ariadne was only four . . ."

Auntie Eva had draped her silk scarf across the chair beside the sideboard. It hung almost to the floor, so Jasmine couldn't see under the chair.

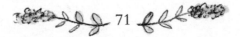

Now, as she scanned the floor beneath the sideboard, the scarf slithered sideways across the chair.

"But then my children were exceptional, of course," Auntie Eva said.

Had the scarf moved, or was she seeing things?

"Tristan was walking at ten months, and Ariadne ..."

The scarf slid to the floor. And there, sitting under the chair, munching on a corner of the silk square, sat a fluffy golden rabbit.

A joyful smile transformed Jasmine's face. Oh, the relief!

"Is something funny?" asked Auntie Eva.

Jasmine hastily rearranged her expression. "No."

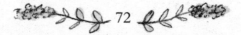

She glanced behind her. "I'll just close these doors. It's a bit drafty, isn't it?"

"Can you never sit still?" asked Auntie Eva. "No wonder you find it hard to learn anything."

The corner of the scarf was disappearing into Daisy's mouth. It would do her no good to swallow it. Jasmine crept across the room toward her.

"What *are* you doing, Jasmine? Is there something wrong with you?" Auntie Eva pushed back her chair. Daisy froze.

Jasmine seized her chance. Dropping to her knees, she reached for the rabbit.

"Aargh!" shrieked Auntie Eva, staring in horror at the furry creature crouched in the shadows.

Daisy bolted across the room. Jasmine lunged for her, toppling the jug from the table. A torrent of water poured into Auntie Eva's lap.

"You clumsy child!" she cried, leaping from her chair. "Look what you've done!"

Then she saw her silk scarf sprawled on the

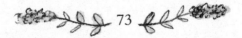

floor, its corner damp and ragged. She screamed in horror.

"Chewed! Chewed to pieces! My best silk scarf!"

Daisy was cowering in the far corner of the room. Jasmine knew the best way to catch an animal was to cover it with a blanket. Before Auntie Eva could terrify poor Daisy any further, Jasmine snatched up the scarf and dropped it over her. She scooped up the trembling animal and held her close. Daisy's heart was pounding.

"It's all right, Daisy," she murmured. "You're safe now."

"My clothes are *completely* ruined," spat Auntie Eva, "and all you seem to care about is that disgusting creature."

"Here's your scarf," said Jasmine. "Sorry about the chewed part."

Auntie Eva recoiled. *"Sorry?"* Then her eye caught something else on the floor. "Ugh!" She stepped back in disgust. Jasmine followed her

gaze and saw a little pile of rabbit droppings on the floor.

"That is absolutely revolting. The conditions here are intolerable. I can't possibly stay the night; I wouldn't get a minute's sleep. I'm calling a taxi to the station immediately."

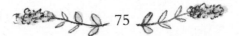

9
You're Safe with Us

"So she actually left?" asked Tom when Jasmine returned to the field.

"Yep. She told Mom and Dad she couldn't possibly stay in a house where rodents were allowed to roam free."

"Were your parents really angry?"

"Well, they didn't actually realize Daisy had escaped. Auntie Evil was too mad to explain it right, and they thought she was talking about the rabbits being in the playpen. And she went on and on about how badly brought up Manu and I are, so I think they were just happy she was leaving."

"That's good that you found Daisy," said Tom.

"I know. I'm so relieved. And she seems fine, thank goodness. Did Storm drink any more milk?"

Tom shook his head. "I think he's pining for his mom. I hope we find her soon."

"Let's make the pen in Mistletoe's shelter," said Jasmine. "Dotty and Truffle will cheer Storm up."

As soon as he walked into the orchard, Storm lifted his head and his ears started swiveling. His nostrils began to quiver.

"It's all right, Storm," said Jasmine soothingly. "You're safe with us."

"I think he can smell something strange," said Tom as he unclipped Mistletoe's lead rope. "Maybe Truffle."

"Truffle won't hurt you, Storm," said Jasmine. "She's very gentle."

"He looks frightened," said Tom. "You said some horses are scared of pigs, didn't you?"

"Nobody could be scared of Truffle."

"I'm not sure. He's really tense."

"Don't worry. We'll introduce them, and then we can check that they get along."

"Storm really doesn't look happy," said Tom anxiously. "Maybe we should take him back to the field."

"Stop fussing. He'll be fine. Dotty! Truffle!"

Dotty scrabbled to her feet and bounded toward her. Truffle heaved herself upright and trotted up the orchard behind the little deer.

Storm stared at the strange animals. He spread his front legs out to the sides and leaned back a little.

"He looks like he might bolt," said Tom. "I think we should take Truffle away."

Storm pawed at the ground with his hoof. Truffle gave a loud grunt. Storm snorted and reared up on his hind legs. Dotty froze. Mistletoe's eyes widened.

Jasmine watched in horror as Storm bolted

across the orchard, snorting and tossing his head.

"Stop, Storm! You'll hurt yourself!"

"Take Truffle away!" said Tom.

Jasmine's heart was pounding. "Truffle! Truffle, come here!"

Truffle didn't move. Storm was galloping around the edge of the orchard, tossing his head and stumbling on his injured leg.

"Get Truffle's food!" shouted Tom.

Of course. Truffle would go anywhere for food. Thank goodness Tom's brain was working, because hers had shut down completely.

Jasmine ran into the garden as another loud snort came from the orchard, followed by a terrible high-pitched squeal.

"Get Truffle away!" yelled Tom.

As though in a nightmare, Jasmine stumbled to the shed, threw a scoop of pignuts into a bucket, and hurtled back to the orchard, rattling the bucket. Out of the corner of her eye she saw Mom run into the garden.

"Truffle!" Jasmine called. "Truffle!"

As she opened the orchard gate, Dotty unfroze and bolted into the path of the terrified foal. With a cry of fear, Tom hurled himself at Dotty. Storm gave a high-pitched squeal, wheeled around, and kicked Tom with the full force of his hind hoof, sending him rolling over on the grass before continuing his sprint around the orchard.

"Tom!" cried Jasmine, racing toward him. But Mom got there first.

"Get Truffle out!" she shouted, dropping to her knees beside Tom.

In a daze of horror, Jasmine rattled the bucket again. Truffle pricked up her ears and trotted toward her. Jasmine backed into the garden, set the bucket down for the pig, and rushed back to the orchard. "Tom!" she cried. "Tom, are you OK?"

Tom lay on the ground. His eyes were open but his face was deathly pale. "Is he OK?" asked Jasmine, ice-cold with fear.

"I'm going to call his mom and take him to the hospital," said Mom.

Jasmine could barely speak. "The hospital?" she whispered.

"He hit his head when he fell and lost consciousness for a few seconds. I'm sure he'll be fine, but we should get it checked out. Shut the gate and watch the foal from the garden. He should calm down now that Truffle's gone. Shut her in the kennel for now."

Mom carried Tom to the house. Wobbly and tearful, Jasmine shut the orchard gate. Why had she been so careless? She'd been so sure the animals would get along together that she'd refused to see the warning signs. Why, oh, why, hadn't she listened to Tom?

10
An Important Lesson

Two hours later, Mom still wasn't back. Storm and Mistletoe stood peacefully together in the orchard. But Jasmine felt far from peaceful. Her head ached and her stomach churned.

What if Tom was badly injured? What if he never recovered? She couldn't bear to think about it.

She would do anything for him to be safe and well. But there was nothing she could do.

If Tom's all right, she thought, *I'll never, ever not listen to him again.*

The sound of Mom's car coming up the drive-way made her heart thump in her chest. Her legs started shaking. Feeling dizzy and sick, she heard the latch rattle on the garden gate and footsteps coming down the path.

Mom looked at Jasmine and said, "Oh, sweet-heart, you look worried to death. It's OK. Tom's going to be fine."

Jasmine stared, unable to take this in.

"They've checked him over and they're keep-ing him for a few hours for observation, but he's going to be fine."

"Oh!" Jasmine gasped. "I thought he was going to die."

Mom pulled her into a hug. "No,

he's had a knock to the head and he's got a massive bruise on his thigh, but he'll be right as rain in no time."

The tension drained out of Jasmine in a huge rush, and she felt as weak as a deflated balloon. She leaned against her mother and sobbed and sobbed and sobbed.

After a rest on the sofa and a mug of hot chocolate, Jasmine told her mom what had happened.

"It was all my fault. He tried to warn me, but I didn't pay any attention."

"Well, you've learned an important lesson about listening," said Mom. "And Tom and Storm are both OK, thank goodness."

"But Storm's limp is worse. And Tom will probably never be allowed to come here again. His parents must hate me."

"I'm sure they don't. Let's go see Storm."

Mistletoe and Storm were standing together in the corner of the orchard, nibbling grass.

"Wow, he's grazing!" said Jasmine. "I didn't know foals started eating grass this young."

"They start tasting it from a couple of weeks," said Mom, "but milk's their main food until they're about six months."

"I'm sure he's not drinking enough milk," said Jasmine. "I think he's pining for his mom."

"Let's put him in the pen," said Mom. "I'll fix a hook to the wall for the bucket, at the same height as a mare's udder."

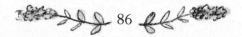

Jasmine led Mistletoe into the pen. Storm hesitated, but then he followed the donkey through the open rail. Jasmine closed it and Mom opened one at the side to lead Mistletoe out.

"Mistletoe will still be here to look after you," Jasmine reassured the foal. "But he won't be able to drink your milk."

While Jasmine stroked and talked to Storm, Mom examined his leg.

"It's more swollen, but his stitches are still intact, thank goodness. He just needs to rest."

Mistletoe nuzzled Storm's mane over the bars of the pen. As Jasmine watched, Dotty walked into the shelter. Jasmine held her breath as Storm turned his head to look at the little deer. They stared at each other for a few seconds, then Storm turned away. Jasmine sighed with relief. He looked perfectly relaxed.

While Mom fixed a hook to the wall, Jasmine mixed a bucket of mare's milk replacement. As she was encouraging Storm to drink, Mom's

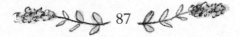

phone rang. Jasmine's stomach churned as she recognized Tom's mom's voice. Was she going to ban Jasmine from seeing him?

Mom walked away a little to take the phone call. When she finished, she said, "There, Jasmine, Miss Mel doesn't hate you."

"What did she say? How's Tom? Is he home?"

"He's home, and he wants to see you. Miss Mel asked if you could pop over after dinner."

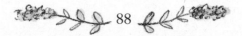

Jasmine felt more and more nervous as she walked across the fields to Tom's house. Why did he want to see her? Was he furious? Did he want to tell her exactly what he thought of her?

When Miss Mel opened the door, Jasmine thought she didn't seem quite as friendly as usual.

"I'm so sorry," Jasmine said. "About Tom. It was all my fault. I didn't listen to him."

"Well, I'm sure you've learned your lesson. And Tom says it was his fault anyway. I'm sure you didn't tell him to run in front of a stampeding horse."

Tom was lying on the sofa, reading something on a laptop. When Jasmine walked in, he closed the computer.

"Hi," he said, smiling at her. He looked pale, but otherwise he seemed his normal self.

"Are you OK?" asked Jasmine. "Does it hurt?"

"It's not too bad. They gave me painkillers and ice. But I'm not allowed to come and help with Storm tomorrow."

"And that's enough time on the computer, too," said Miss Mel, picking up the laptop.

"But I need to do more research."

"You can do more tomorrow," she said as she left the room. "You need to go to bed after Jasmine leaves."

"How's Storm?" Tom asked as Jasmine sat down.

"Much better. He's in the pen now. He and Dotty seem fine together. I'm not sure what we're going to do about Truffle, though." She paused. "You were so brave, protecting Dotty.

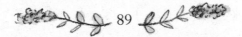

Imagine if she'd been kicked in the head." She shuddered at the thought. "I'm really sorry I didn't listen to you."

"You should always listen to me," said Tom. "I'm very wise."

Jasmine laughed, and for the first time she felt better. Everything was going to be all right.

"What were you researching?" she asked.

"Different stuff. I found a great site about horse markings. All the marks have different names. That

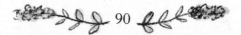

white mark above Storm's hoof on his left fore-leg is called a pastern, and the thin white stripe above his right hoof is a coronet. Then I looked up abandoned foals. There were lots of news-paper articles about people finding foals dumped in fields and stuff."

"Oh, we should phone the local paper!" said Jasmine. "They could do an article about him with a picture, and someone might recognize him. I'll ask Mom to phone them tomorrow."

"Has he drunk any more milk?" asked Tom.

"A little bit, but not enough. I'm sure he's pin-ing for his mom. He was whinnying, which must be him calling to her. It's really sad."

"But if he was abandoned, he won't be able to go back, will he?" said Tom. "His owners obvi-ously didn't want him if they abandoned him."

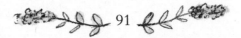

As Jasmine walked home across the fields, she was a jumble of emotions. By far the best thing for Storm would be for him to be reunited with his mother, but it seemed most likely that he had been abandoned. If he had been, would he ever recover from being separated from his mom? And where would he live if he couldn't go back to her? Was there any chance that her parents would let him stay?

11
You're Never Satisfied

"Can we phone the local paper about Storm?" Jasmine asked her mom at breakfast the next morning. She had already taken fresh milk to Storm and spent an hour playing with the rabbits.

"That's a good idea," said Mom. "I'll do it tomorrow. I won't have time today because we're TB testing."

All the cows had to be tested for tuberculosis by a vet every year. Mom always did the testing at Oak Tree Farm.

On the first day of the testing week, she gave each cow two injections. Three days later, she checked them to see if they had reacted to the injections. Today she was checking for responders. If a cow had responded, that meant it had TB and would have to be put down.

Tuberculosis was a very infectious disease, and if even one cow on the farm had it, then Dad would have to keep almost all of the farm animals for at least sixty days. That meant he wouldn't get any money from selling animals, and he would have to spend more money to keep feeding them. So the day that Mom checked for responders was always stressful. Jasmine had learned it was best to keep out of the way.

When she went back to the orchard, she was glad to see Storm had drunk some of the milk, though not as much as she would have liked. She tried to encourage him to take more, but he wouldn't be persuaded.

"Let's go out to the field," she said, taking Mistletoe's halter from its hook.

Dotty followed Mistletoe to the gate. "You want to come, too, don't you?" said Jasmine, stroking the little deer's head. "But I'll let Truffle out in a minute, so you'll have company in here."

In the field, she unclipped Mistletoe's lead rope and turned to Storm. He sniffed her hand and she stroked his mane and cheek.

"Your leg looks better. It's much less swollen. And you look more relaxed. I think it did you good to spend the night in the pen with Mistletoe babysitting you."

Storm nuzzled her hand, and then he started trotting around the field, flicking his tail. He trotted up to Mistletoe, nuzzled his mouth, and reared up on his hind legs. Mistletoe lowered his head to graze, ignoring the foal.

"He's asking you to play, Mistletoe," said Jasmine. "Go on, play with him." Storm flicked his tail and trotted in a wide circle around Mistletoe, jumping and kicking his back legs in the air. Then he trotted back and nuzzled him again. Mistletoe still ignored him. But after Storm came and nuzzled him a third time, Mistletoe followed him when he started trotting around the field.

"Oh, you're playing! Well done, Storm—you've finally persuaded him."

As she watched them playing, an exciting vision started to form in her head. A gleaming, white-washed stable, with Storm looking out over the door of his cozy stall. Next to the stall, she would keep all his tack and equipment: his saddle and bridle, his blankets, his grooming kit. And when he was old enough, they could canter all over the countryside together.

"If we can't find your owners," Jasmine said as she stroked his soft ears, "or if your owners don't want you, I'll look after you—I promise. You'd be happy here with me and Mistletoe, wouldn't you, Storm?"

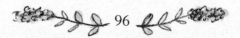

"The police just phoned," said Mom when Jasmine went inside for dinner. "The RSPCA inspected those stables in Ryewell yesterday and they found nothing wrong."

Jasmine frowned. "But why did their neighbor report them, then? They must have been doing something."

"Well, apparently the neighbor has had a long-running quarrel with the stables' owners about a property line. It looks as though she's trying to get them in trouble out of spite. And the RSPCA checked with the vet the stables use, and he confirmed that the number of horses and foals they have is exactly what they should have."

"So Storm didn't come from there."

"No. And none of the other people I contacted knows anything about Storm, either. So we'll have to keep searching."

They were having Jasmine's favorite curry for

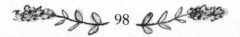

dinner, and what with enjoying the meal and thinking about Storm, she wasn't paying attention to the conversation.

"I can't believe it," Dad was saying. "It's just one thing after another right now."

"But only one cow has TB," said Manu. "So why's it so bad?"

"Because we can't move any animals on or off the farm for at least sixty days. Maybe a lot longer if other cows catch it. All the calves that were ready to be sold next week will have to stay, and all the new ones I was about to buy won't be able to come."

"Thank goodness it's nearly summer, at least," said Mom, "and they can be out in the fields, not costing a fortune to feed in the barn."

"For the moment, yes, but this could drag on all winter."

Mom sighed. "How was the foal today, Jasmine?"

"Amazing," said Jasmine. "He's so friendly now, and he and Mistletoe really love each other. I was thinking, if he's been abandoned and his owners don't want him, could he stay here? We could turn one of the old cow stalls into a stable, couldn't we, Dad? I could clear it out and paint it."

Dad didn't reply. He was eating absentmindedly, his head bent to the table.

"Dad?" said Jasmine.

"What?"

"Storm's stable," said Jasmine patiently. "He's fine in Mistletoe's shelter for now, but he'll need his own stable when he's bigger."

"Jasmine, this isn't a good time," said Mom. "Dad's had a tough day and he's tired."

Dad looked up, frowning. "Are you asking to keep another animal, Jasmine?"

"Only Storm. He'd be perfect for me. I've always wanted to ride, and Mistletoe's too old. And he'll be a great companion for Mistletoe."

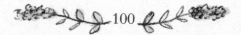

"Don't you already have a deer and a pig as companions for Mistletoe? And I thought the foal didn't get along with Truffle."

"He just needs time to get used to her. Honestly, Dad, it wouldn't be any extra trouble."

Dad's face was growing red, which was never a good sign. "No extra trouble? Do you have any idea how much it costs to keep a horse?"

"But Mom would do his injections and checks and everything, and we wouldn't have to pay for bedding or feed or grazing, and—"

"Oh, so all those things will magically fall into your lap, will they?"

"No, but . . . I mean, we have them all here, so . . ."

Dad pushed back his chair and stood up. "So all that means nothing, does it? Feed, bedding, grazing, veterinary care, all free? When will you learn to appreciate what you've got, Jasmine, and not keep constantly asking for more? You've added a deer and a donkey in the past year alone, but

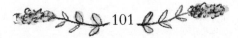

you're never satisfied, are you? You're behaving so selfishly."

He strode out of the room, leaving the others sitting in a horrible silence.

Jasmine stared down at the table. She picked up her fork, but the curry didn't taste good anymore, and she couldn't eat it.

12
All Wrong

Jasmine sat on her bed, seething with anger. How dare Dad call her selfish! And Mom hadn't even stood up for her. Just because they were stressed about the TB tests didn't mean they had the right to take it out on her. All she had done was care for a poor abandoned foal. They were acting as though she was selfish and spoiled, when she was just trying to give an unwanted animal a loving home.

They'll be sorry, she thought. *When Storm and I win the Grand National, and I get interviewed on TV,*

I'll tell them how mean my parents were, and how they wouldn't even let me have a horse.

She had planned to stay in her room all evening, to show her parents how much they had hurt her, but she soon realized this wasn't possible. Sky would need his evening walk, Dotty and Truffle had to be fed, Truffle had to be put in the kennel, Mistletoe and Storm needed to be brought into the shelter, and she wanted to play with the rabbits. So she heaved herself off her bed and stomped downstairs to put her boots on.

"He's so mean," she said to Sky as he bounded joyfully through the fields. "Can you believe he called me selfish? As though it's selfish to care for animals! Well if that's true, then he's the most selfish one of all. Look how many animals he's got. Hundreds of cows and sheep and chickens, and nobody bothers *him* about it."

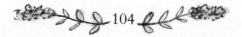

Jasmine woke up the next morning with a heavy heart. Not only were her parents mean and unreasonable, but she had to go to a birthday party this afternoon.

"Do I *have* to go?" she asked her mother when she went downstairs for breakfast.

"Yes. You accepted the invitation, and it would be rude to back out now."

"But it's such a waste of time. And Bella Bradley's going to be there." Bella Bradley was in Jasmine's class, and she and Jasmine did not get along. Bella really *was* selfish, thought Jasmine. How dare her parents say they were anything alike! She was absolutely nothing like Bella.

Just after three o'clock, Jasmine stood on the doorstep of Sophie's house, wearing clean clothes and holding a present. She forced a smile as Sophie opened the door.

"Happy birthday," she said, handing Sophie the present.

"Thank you," said Sophie. "We're decorating cookies in the kitchen."

The boys were sitting on one side of the big

kitchen table, and the girls were on the other. Tom and some of the others said hello to Jasmine. Bella Bradley sat in the center of the line of girls. She had selected a gingerbread man, and now she was examining the decorations. She glanced at Jasmine, took a sneering look at her clothes, and turned back to her friends.

"I'm getting my room redecorated," she said, reaching for the chocolate chips. "I'm having all new furniture. Everything white. A bed and a desk and a wardrobe and a chest of drawers. And I'm going to have new curtains and get it all repainted. Pass the silver balls, Aisha."

"Oh, wow, it will look amazing," said Sadie.

"Didn't you just get all new furniture?" said Zara.

"Like two years ago," said Bella dismissively. "I hate it now. It's really babyish."

"You're so lucky," said Millie. "My bed's really ugly, but my mom won't get me a new one."

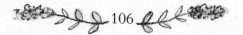

"You have to persuade them," said Bella. "Mine said no at first, but I just kept asking. They always give in eventually. Just act really sad when they say no, and then be really nice and sweet to them until you get what you want."

Standing on her own at the end of the table, Jasmine suddenly felt very uncomfortable. Was she more like Bella than she wanted to believe?

She and Tom didn't get the chance to talk until the birthday dinner, when Jasmine managed to sit next to him.

"How's your head?" she asked.

"Fine," said Tom through a mouthful of pizza. "Hey, guess what? I found an online site where people post if their horse has gone missing."

Jasmine's stomach tightened. "Was Storm on it?"

"No, but it was interesting reading the stories. Some of them were really sad. Someone had posted a picture of their palomino foal that was stolen from its field. They said the mare was really distressed; she was calling constantly for him and they couldn't comfort her at all. But tons of people shared the post and someone recognized the foal. The thieves had been trying to sell him hundreds of miles away."

"Did they get him back?"

"Yes, there was a really cute video of him being reunited with his mom. They were so happy to see each other. They sniffed each other all over, and then they started running around the field together."

Sophie's mom walked in, carrying a huge

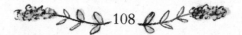

chocolate cake with lit candles. They all sang "Happy Birthday" and then Tom started talking to Marco. Jasmine was left with her thoughts.

What if Storm had been stolen? Mom had made inquiries in the local area, but what if he had come from much farther away? What if he had a mother who was missing him terribly?

But if he'd been stolen, why had he ended up on her farm? It didn't make sense. Thieves would have kept him or sold him, wouldn't they?

But what if he'd been stolen and then abandoned afterward? Perhaps he'd been injured while the thieves were transporting him, and they'd abandoned him because they couldn't sell him with an injured leg. Or maybe they'd discovered the police were after them, so they'd dumped him on the farm to get rid of the evidence.

With a flash of guilt, Jasmine realized that she had been telling herself that Storm had been orphaned or abandoned by his owners not because those were the most likely things to have

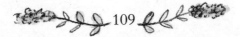

happened, but because that was what she wanted to think. She had believed what she wanted to believe, because she wanted to keep Storm for herself. And that was all wrong.

She should have been thinking about what was best for Storm. Her job was to try to find out where he had come from, not just selfishly hope he was an unwanted orphan.

She turned to Tom. "On that lost-and-stolen horses site," she said, "can you post if you've found a foal?"

"I think so. Yes, there was a post about a horse someone had found."

"Then we should post a picture of Storm. We have to do everything we can to find his mother."

13
Sunny

Tom and Jasmine decided they should go to her house to use the website, so Mom picked them both up from the party.

"Tom's found a site for lost-and-found horses," said Jasmine. "Will you help us post a picture of Storm on it?"

Mom gave her an approving look. "That's a very good idea. I should have thought of it myself."

Tom took lots of pictures of Storm, and they chose the best ones to post on the site.

"What if someone makes a false claim, though?" he asked.

Jasmine looked at Mom in alarm. "Yes! Someone could lie and say he's theirs, just to get a free foal."

"Don't worry," said Mom. "I'll ask plenty of questions. And if somebody's foal has gone missing, they should have reported it to the local police, so I'll check with them. Besides, I'm sure his owner will have photos of him, so we can ask to see them."

Jasmine looked at the pictures they'd selected. "Let's not post this one. It's the only one that shows his whole body. If we don't use any photos that show below his knees, we can ask anyone who says they're his owner to describe his markings. If they know he's got a white pastern on his left foreleg and a white coronet on his right foreleg as well as the socks on his hind legs, then we'll know they're his real owner."

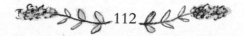

"Excellent thinking, Jasmine," said Mom. "You should be a detective."

Tom and Jasmine checked the site as soon as they met up the next day. Some people had shared the post and there were a few messages saying what a lovely foal he was and hoping he would soon be reunited with his mom. But nobody had recognized him or had any idea where he might have come from.

"It's probably too soon," said Tom. "We only posted it last night."

After they had fed the animals, walked Sky, and played with Buster and Daisy, they fetched Mistletoe and Storm to take them to the field.

"He drank more milk last night," said Jasmine, looking into the bucket. "That's a good sign."

Tom led Mistletoe while Jasmine walked behind with Storm, carrying a big beach ball. Last night they had watched videos of foals playing

with balls, and she was excited to see what Storm
would make of it.

In the field, she placed the ball in front of him.
He stared at the strange new object.

"Do you want to play with it?" she asked.
"Look what it can do."

She rolled the ball away from him. Storm
stared at it for a second. Then he nudged
it experimentally with his nose. The ball

rolled forward. Storm walked after it. He pawed
it with his hoof and nudged it forward again.

"I think he likes it," said Jasmine, grinning
at Tom.

They laughed as Storm nipped at the ball,
trying and failing to get a grip on the shiny
surface. The ball rolled forward and he ran
after it.

"Look!" said Tom. "He's dribbling it!"

Storm reared up and tried to plant his front feet on the moving ball, but he ended up splayed over it, the ball trapped between his forelegs and his hind legs. Tom laughed and went to dislodge it, but Jasmine pulled him back.

"I'll do it. Don't go near his hooves."

After half an hour, Storm lay down for a nap. Jasmine went to let Truffle out of the kennel. She scrabbled to her feet, grunting in greeting.

"Poor Truffle. You don't like sleeping on your own, do you? Come to the orchard and see Dotty."

At lunchtime, Jasmine and Tom went inside to make sandwiches, play with the rabbits, and check the lost-and-found site. Their post had been shared over two hundred times.

"That's good," said Tom. "Lots of people are trying to help."

Jasmine read the comments. Everyone was very supportive, but still nobody had recognized Storm.

"Poor Storm," she said. "He must have an owner somewhere."

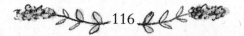

At that moment, the phone rang. Mom and Dad were both out working, so Jasmine answered it.

"Hello?" said a man's voice. "Could I speak to Dr. Singh?"

"She's out at the moment. This is her daughter. Can I take a message?"

"Could you let her know it's my foal she's found? He went missing from my field three days ago. He's only three weeks old and we've been beside ourselves with worry. My little girl's distraught. I can't tell you how relieved I was to see that picture. We're so grateful to you. If you give me your address, I'll come and fetch him."

Jasmine had thought she would be thrilled to find Storm's owner. But all she felt was that she didn't want to hand Storm over to this stranger.

But she was being selfish, wasn't she? She just didn't want to say goodbye to Storm.

"OK," she said. "When will you be coming?"

"That depends where you are. If you're local, I could come this afternoon. What's your address?"

Tom shook his head. "Ask about his markings," he mouthed.

"Uh, can you tell me about his markings?" asked Jasmine. "Just so we know it's the right foal."

The man laughed. "Of course it's the right foal. He's got a white blaze. I recognized him right away. I'd know him anywhere. Just tell me your address so I can fetch him."

Tom shook his head warningly. He took out his phone and held it up to the landline, recording the conversation.

"Can you tell me what other markings your foal has?" asked Jasmine.

"I've got several foals. I couldn't tell you exactly what markings this one has."

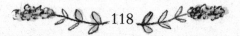

Tom's presence made Jasmine braver. "I'm sorry," she said, "but we need to know that we're handing him to the right owner before we can tell you the address."

"So you won't give my foal back?"

"We will as soon as you can tell us his markings. Ask your little girl. I'm sure she'll know."

Tom grinned and gave her a thumbs-up.

The man's voice sounded threatening now. "So you're refusing to hand back my foal? That's stealing, you know. I'll report this to the police."

He hung up.

Jasmine stared at Tom. She felt a bit sick.

"Wow," said Tom as he stopped recording. "He was definitely lying. Let's write down his number. Then your mom can report *him* to the police."

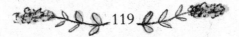

After lunch, they walked Sky before returning to the field to spend the afternoon with Storm and Mistletoe. When they went back inside and checked the site again, there was still nothing.

"I wonder if Mom's contacted the local paper," said Jasmine. "She said she'd do it today and send them a photo."

"If she did, they might have already written the article," said Tom. "Let's have a look."

He typed "Missing Foals" into the search engine. Jasmine scanned the results. Her eyes came to rest on a headline.

Weeks–Old Missing Foal Will Die without Its Mother, Says Heartbroken Owner

Her heart started thumping. "Look!"

Tom clicked on the headline. The page loaded and a photo came into view.

Tom gasped.

The foal had two white socks on its hind legs, a white pastern on its left foreleg, and a white coronet on its right foreleg.

"It is him, isn't it?" said Tom. "It's definitely Storm."

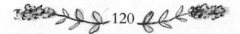

Jasmine couldn't speak. She read the article. It was from a newspaper called the *North Yorkshire News*, and it had just been posted that morning.

Weeks-Old Missing Foal
Will Die without Its Mother,
Says Heartbroken Owner

A three-week-old foal has vanished from a field in Pilbury, and his heartbroken owner says he won't survive without his mother.

Sunny was last seen by his owner on Monday, May 25. He went missing from a field at Broadlands Farm, where he lived with his mom, Athena.

"I checked them at 7 p.m. and they were in the field together," said owner Jane Stanford. "But when I went out to feed Athena on Tuesday morning, Sunny had disappeared."

Jane and her daughter, Lola, searched the farm, but they found no trace of the little foal.

"There were tire tracks leading to the field," said Jane, "which look like they were made by a truck. We've searched everywhere. If he was lost, we would have heard him and his mom calling to each other, and if he'd died, we'd have found the body."

They reported the disappearance to police, but are hoping that if someone took Sunny, they will return him to the field.

"We're heartbroken," said Jane, who has also spoken to local radio. "His mom is lost

without him. She was absolutely devoted to him and he won't survive for long without her, unless he's with someone who knows how to take care of foals. We just want him back."

She added, "My daughter is so upset. We can't understand why someone would do this. We keep going to the field to look for him. It's just devastating."

Anyone who has seen Sunny is asked to report it to the police at the following number.

Tom and Jasmine stared at the screen in silence. Then Tom said, "We need to call that number."

14
Everything I Need

The next afternoon, Jasmine and Tom led Mistletoe and Storm into the field pen. Then Jasmine clipped on Mistletoe's lead rope. It wouldn't be a good idea for him to be there when Storm was reunited with his mother.

"Say goodbye to Storm," she said to him. "You've been an amazing foster parent. We couldn't have looked after him without you."

"I'm glad they're bringing Storm's mom to meet him," said Tom when Jasmine returned from the orchard. "It would be awful for him to travel all that way on his own."

"Especially when his last journey must have been so horrible. Poor Storm. No wonder he was terrified when I first saw him."

"I suppose we should call him Sunny now."

Jasmine wrinkled her nose. "Storm's a much better name."

"What if his mom rejects him?"

Jasmine was worried about this, too, but she didn't want to show it. "She won't. Horses can recognize each other after years apart, so she'll definitely know him after a few days."

"It's lucky that horses aren't included in the quarantine rules," said Tom. "That would be—"

"Look!" said Jasmine. "They're here."

A blue SUV trundled slowly up the driveway, towing a horse trailer.

Jasmine felt a whirl of emotions. Part of her wanted to hold on to Storm and never let him go. But another part of her was very proud that she

and Tom were reuniting the mare and her foal. And she was excited to see how Storm would react when he saw his mother again.

"We'd better go meet them," she said.

The SUV stopped next to the field gate as they approached. A woman got out of the driver's door. Then the passenger door opened and a girl about Jasmine's age appeared.

The girl saw the foal in the pen and squealed with excitement. "It's Sunny! Oh, Mom, look, it's Sunny!"

Her mom's face lit up with joy as she saw the foal. She beamed at Jasmine and Tom. "I don't know how to thank you. We've been so worried, and to find him safe and sound . . . It's amazing!"

"Can we let Athena out?" asked the girl. "I can't wait to see them together again."

"Of course," said her mom. "I'm Ms. Stanford, by the way. And this is my daughter, Lola. You must be Jasmine."

"Yes, and this is Tom. He's been looking after Storm, too."

"Storm?" said Ms. Stanford and Lola together.

Jasmine felt her cheeks burning. "Sorry. We didn't know his name, so . . . There was a storm on the night he arrived, you see."

"That's so funny that we called him Sunny and you called him Storm," said Lola.

"Would you mind taking the pen away while we unload Athena?" Ms. Stanford said. "I have a feeling they're going to want to be together the second they see each other, and we don't want either of them injured."

"Sure," said Jasmine. She and Tom walked back to Storm's pen. Jasmine climbed inside. She put her arms around Storm and laid her cheek against his.

"I'm going to miss you so much," she said, blinking back the tears that threatened to fall. "You're the sweetest foal ever, and it's been amazing getting to know you. But your mom's here now, and that's what matters. You're going back home with your mom, Storm. Isn't that lovely?"

She wiped her cheeks with the back of her hand and helped Tom dismantle the pen. As they carried the rails out of the gate, Ms. Stanford led a beautiful chestnut mare out of the horse trailer. She had a white star above her eyes and, like Storm, two white socks on her hind legs.

"Oh, she's gorgeous!" said Jasmine. "What a lovely horse."

At the open gate, Ms. Stanford unclipped Athena's lead rope and stood back. Storm had his head down, sniffing the grass. The mare looked straight at her foal and gave a loud whinny. Storm lifted his head, pricked his ears forward, and looked at her. He gave a loud whinny in reply. Athena cantered toward him, neighing again. She slowed to a halt in front of him and bent her head to sniff his neck. She made a low-pitched, guttural noise that sounded to Jasmine like an expression of complete happiness.

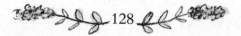

"Oh, she's nickering to him," murmured Lola.

"Is that what that sound's called?" asked Jasmine.

"Yes, mares nicker to call their foals, and also when they're happy. Listen, she's grunting with contentment, too."

Athena nuzzled Storm's neck. Storm moved closer to her, until they were standing cheek to cheek. They stood like that for a long time,

making gentle low-pitched sounds and blowing softly. Then Storm moved to Athena's hind legs and began to drink.

"Oh!" exclaimed Jasmine softly. "He must be so happy to have his mom's milk again."

Athena turned her head to nuzzle her foal. She clearly couldn't get enough of his presence. As he drank, she licked and sniffed and nuzzled him continually.

Jasmine noticed Mom walking toward them.

"What a beautiful sight," she said as she drew close. "Hello, I'm Nadia. You must be Jane and Lola."

Ms. Stanford's eyes were shiny with tears. "Oh, Nadia, I don't know how to thank you. I can't believe Sunny ended up on a farm with a vet to look after him. We're so lucky he found you."

"Well, Jasmine and Tom did most of the work. They're excellent animal rescuers."

"But how did he end up here?" asked Jasmine. "Do you know what happened?"

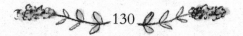

"Actually, I just had a call from the police," Mom said. "They said they'd tried to call you first, Jane, but they couldn't get through, so they called me."

"What did they say?" asked Jasmine.

"Someone who works the night shift at a gas station in the Midlands had seen our post online. She saw the picture and remembered that a truck had stopped at the gas station in the middle of the night on Monday. The driver opened the back to put something in, and she'd glimpsed a foal's face and heard it neighing. She said the driver slammed the door and drove off in a big hurry, and it all seemed very odd, but she didn't think any more about it until she saw the post. Then she checked her CCTV footage and found the truck's license plate. She reported it to the police and it turned out they'd had their eye on the truck's owner for a while. He was suspected of being involved in other crimes in the area, but they didn't have enough evidence to arrest him.

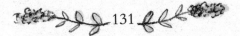

But his face was caught on the CCTV at the gas station, and there's clear footage of Storm—sorry, Sunny—in the back of the truck."

"So they've arrested him?" asked Jasmine.

"They have. Well done, you two. You've solved a crime and reunited a foal and his mother."

"But that doesn't explain why he ended up here."

"Well, it looks as though the thief was planning to sell him, but when Sunny got injured the buyer wouldn't take him anymore, so he abandoned him."

"How lucky that he left him here," said Ms. Stanford. "Otherwise I dread to think what might have happened."

Storm had finished drinking, and the two horses were nuzzling each other again. Suddenly Storm kicked up his heels and galloped away. Athena ran after him, and they raced around the field together, Athena letting her son lead but staying right beside him.

Lola turned to her mom. "I think we should give him Storm as a middle name."

"Sunny Storm?" said Jasmine.

"Yes. He's had good and bad times in his life, so he should have sun and storm in his name."

Ms. Stanford took a business card out of her pocket. "We've got a vacation cottage on the farm that we rent out," she said, handing the card to Jasmine. "We'd love for you and your family to come and stay. And your friend, of course," she said, smiling at Tom. "It sleeps eight, so there's plenty of room. Any week that suits you, just let me know. As a gift, of course—a small token to thank you for looking after Sunny. And I give riding lessons, so you can ride every day if you'd like to. Athena is one of our riding mares."

"Oh, wow," said Jasmine. "That would be amazing. Can we, Mom?"

"It sounds wonderful," said Mom. "Thank you very much indeed. We'd love to come."

A loud grunt came from the orchard. "Do you have pigs?" asked Ms. Stanford.

"Just one," said Jasmine. "She's called Truffle."

"It's lucky Sunny didn't meet her. He got chased by a pig just after he was born. He's terrified of them."

"Really?" said Jasmine, and she and Tom shot each other a look. But they said nothing.

When it was time for the horses to leave, Jasmine and Tom said a sad goodbye to the little foal.

"We're coming to visit you soon," said Jasmine, stroking his neck lovingly. "We'll see you during vacation. Have a lovely trip home."

They watched until the trailer was out of sight. Then they walked back to the house.

Neither of them spoke until they reached the farmyard. Then Tom said, "Let's go see the rabbits."

Manu was already in the playpen, feeding apple slices to Daisy and Buster. Tom and Jasmine climbed in. Jasmine scooped Buster into her arms and laid her cheek against his warm fur.

"You are so cute. And so fluffy."

Tom rolled a ball for Daisy, who scampered after it, pounced, and tried to bite it. Tom laughed. "Just like Storm did with the beach ball," he said.

Jasmine sighed and stroked Buster's ears.

"It would have been lovely to have a foal, but I guess I'm pretty lucky already."

"You certainly are," said Dad.

She turned to see him smiling from the doorway.

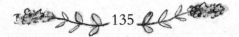

"I came to tell you dinner's ready. And there's ice cream for dessert. I know it's not the same as having a foal of your own, but it's something. And you two did a great job, tracking down the foal's owners *and* thwarting a kidnapping attempt. Mom reported the phone call you recorded, and that man will be getting a visit from the police. Maybe you ought to go into detective work."

"We're going to run an animal rescue center," said Jasmine. "You know that."

Dad gestured to the rabbits and then out of the window toward the orchard, where Mistletoe, Dotty, and Truffle were snuggled together under an apple tree. "It looks like you already do," he said.

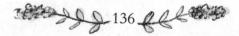

"I'm sorry about the TB test," said Jasmine as they walked to the kitchen.

"Don't worry. We'll deal with it."

"You don't have to get me anything for Christmas if you're short on money. I've got everything I need."

Dad laughed.

"Why are you laughing? I mean it!"

"I know you do. You always mean it, right up until the moment you find another animal. You mean it every single time."

About the Creators

Helen Peters is the author of numerous books for young readers that feature heroic girls saving the day on farms. She grew up on an old-fashioned farm in England, surrounded by family, animals, and mud. Helen Peters lives in East Sussex, England.

Ellie Snowdon is a children's author–illustrator from a tiny village in South Wales. She received her MA in children's book illustration at Cambridge School of Art. Ellie Snowdon lives in Cambridge, England.